My Emotions
EMBARRASSED

AMY CULLIFORD

A Crabtree Roots Book

Crabtree Publishing
crabtreebooks.com

School-to-Home Support for Caregivers and Teachers

This book helps children grow by letting them practice reading. Here are a few guiding questions to help the reader with building his or her comprehension skills. Possible answers appear here in red.

Before Reading:

- What do I think this book is about?
  - *I think this book is about emotions.*
  - *I think this book is about feeling embarrassed.*

- What do I want to learn about this topic?
  - *I want to learn about how to deal with feeling embarrassed.*
  - *I want to learn more about my other emotions.*

During Reading:

- I wonder why…
  - *I wonder why some people laugh at others.*
  - *I wonder why some people look down when they feel embarrassed.*

- What have I learned so far?
  - *I have learned that embarrassed is an emotion.*
  - *I have learned that I might blush when I'm embarrassed.*

After Reading:

- What details did I learn about this topic?
  - *I have learned that writing down my emotions can help me feel better.*
  - *I have learned that it can help to talk about my emotions.*

- Read the book again and look for the vocabulary words.
  - *I see the word **embarrassed** on page 3 and the word **laugh** on page 6. The other vocabulary words are found on page 14.*

Embarrassed is an **emotion**.

I feel embarrassed when I make a **mistake**.

I feel embarrassed when people **laugh** at me.

I look down when I feel embarrassed.

I **blush** when I feel embarrassed.

I want to hide when
I feel embarrassed.

It can help to write down your emotions.

It can help to **talk** to someone when you feel embarrassed.

Word List
Sight Words

an	I	someone	your
at	is	to	
can	it	want	
down	look	when	
help	me	write	
hide	people	you	

Words to Know

blush

embarrassed

emotion

laugh

mistake

talk

60 Words

Embarrassed is an **emotion**.

I feel embarrassed when I make a **mistake**.

I feel embarrassed when people **laugh** at me.

I look down when I feel embarrassed.

I **blush** when I feel embarrassed.

I want to hide when I feel embarrassed.

It can help to write down your emotions.

It can help to talk to someone when you feel embarrassed.

My Emotions
EMBARRASSED

Written by: Amy Culliford
Designed by: Rhea Wallace
Series Development: James Earley
Proofreader: Janine Deschenes
Educational Consultant: Marie Lemke M.Ed.

Photographs:
Shutterstock: Anderson Piza: p. 1; Marongrit Lokoolprakit: p. 3; Westock Productions: p. 5; LightField Studios: p. 7; TheVisualsYouNeed: p. 9; fizkes: p. 10;We_bubble168: p. 11; SynthEx: p. 12; Andrey_popov: p. 13

Crabtree Publishing

crabtreebooks.com   800-387-7650
Copyright © 2023 Crabtree Publishing
All rights reserved. No part of this publication may be reproduced, stored in a retrieval system or be transmitted in any form or by any means, electronic, mechanical, photocopying, recording, or otherwise, without the prior written permission of Crabtree Publishing.

Printed in the U.S.A./012023/
CG20220815

Published in Canada
Crabtree Publishing
616 Welland Ave.
St. Catharines, Ontario
L2M 5V6

Published in the United States
Crabtree Publishing
347 Fifth Ave
Suite 1402-145
New York, NY 10016

Library and Archives Canada Cataloguing in Publication
Available at Library and Archives Canada

Library of Congress Cataloging-in-Publication Data
Available at the Library of Congress

Hardcover: 978-1-0396-9637-2
Paperback: 978-1-0396-9744-7
Ebook (pdf): 978-1-0396-9958-8
Epub: 978-1-0396-9851-2